The Velveteen Rabbit

Adapted from the story by Margery Williams

Illustrated by Judith Sutton

A GOLDEN BOOK · NEW YORK

Western Publishing Company, Inc., Racine, Wisconsin 53404

There was once a velveteen rabbit, and in the beginning he was really splendid. He was fat and bunchy. His coat was brown and white, and his ears were lined with pink sateen. On Christmas morning he sat wedged in the top of the Boy's stocking, with a sprig of holly between his paws.

For at least two hours the Boy loved him, and then in the excitement of looking at all the new presents, the Velveteen Rabbit was forgotten.

For a long time the Velveteen Rabbit lived in the toy cupboard in the nursery. He was naturally shy, and some of the more expensive toys snubbed him.

The mechanical toys were very superior and pretended they were real. Even the jointed wooden lion put on airs.

Only the Skin Horse was kind to the Velveteen Rabbit. The Skin Horse was very wise and had lived longer in the nursery than any of the other toys. He knew that nursery magic is very strange and wonderful, and only those playthings that are very old and experienced can understand it.

"What is REAL?" the Rabbit asked the Skin Horse one day. "Does it mean having things that buzz inside you and a stick-out handle?"

"Real isn't how you are made," said the Skin Horse. "It's a thing that happens to you. It takes a long, long time. That's why it doesn't often happen to toys that break easily, or who have sharp edges, or have to be carefully kept. When a child REALLY loves you, then you become Real."

"I suppose you are REAL?" asked the Rabbit.

The Skin Horse smiled. "The Boy's uncle made me Real many years ago," he said. "And once you are Real, you can't become unreal again. It lasts for always."

The Rabbit sighed. He thought it would be a long
time before this magic thing called Real happened to him.

One evening, when the Boy was going to bed, he couldn't find the toy dog that always slept with him. So Nana gave him the Velveteen Rabbit instead.

That night, and for many nights after, the Velveteen Rabbit slept in the Boy's bed.

At first the Rabbit found it rather uncomfortable. Then he grew to like it, for the Boy made nice tunnels for him under the bedclothes. The Boy said they were like the burrows the real rabbits lived in. And when the Boy dropped off to sleep, the Rabbit would snuggle down under the Boy's warm little chin and dream.

And so time went on. The little Rabbit was so happy that he never noticed how his beautiful velveteen fur was getting shabbier, and his tail was coming unsewn, and all the pink was rubbing off his nose where the Boy kissed him.

When Spring came, the Rabbit had rides in the wheelbarrow, picnics on the grass, and fairy huts built just for him under the raspberry bush.

And once when the Boy was called away suddenly, and the Rabbit was left out on the lawn until long after dusk, Nana had to go and look for him because the Boy couldn't sleep unless he was there.

"Fancy all that fuss for a toy!" said Nana.

The Boy sat up in bed. "He isn't a toy," he said. "He's REAL!"

When the little Rabbit heard that, he was happy, for he knew that what the Skin Horse had said was true at last. He was a toy no longer. He was Real! The Boy himself had said so.

One summer evening the Rabbit saw two strange beings creep out of the woods. They were rabbits like himself, but quite furry and brand new. They must have been very well made, for their seams didn't show, and they changed shape when they moved.

They stared at him, and the little Rabbit stared back. And all the time their noses twitched.

"Why don't you get up and play with us?" one of them asked.

"I don't feel like it," said the Velveteen Rabbit.

"Can you hop on your hind legs?" asked the other furry rabbit.

"I don't want to," answered the Velveteen Rabbit.

One of the rabbits came up very close and sniffed.
"He hasn't got any hind legs!" the furry rabbit called
out. "And he doesn't smell right! He isn't a rabbit at all!
He isn't real!"

"I *am* Real!" said the little Rabbit. "The Boy said so!"

But just then there was a sound of footsteps, and the Boy ran past the furry rabbits. With a stamp of feet and a flash of white, the two strange rabbits disappeared.

For a long time the little Rabbit sat very still, hoping the two rabbits would come back to play with him. But they never returned. The sun sank lower, and the Boy came to carry him home.

Then one day the Boy grew ill. His face grew flushed, he talked in his sleep, and his little body was so hot that it burned the Rabbit when he held him close.

It was a long, weary time, for the Boy was too ill to play. But the little Rabbit snuggled down patiently and looked forward to the time when they would play in the garden and the wood like they used to.

At last the fever turned, and the Boy got better. The doctor ordered that all the books and toys that the Boy had played with be burned. So the little Rabbit was put into a sack and carried out to the garden.

Nearby he could see the raspberry bush that he had played in with the Boy. He thought of the Skin Horse and all that he had been told by him. Of what use was it to be loved and become Real if it all ended like this? And a tear, a real tear, trickled down his shabby velvet nose and fell to the ground.

And then a strange thing happened. For where the tear had fallen, a flower grew out of the ground. And out of that flower stepped a fairy. She came close to the little Rabbit and kissed him on his velveteen nose.

"Little Rabbit, don't you know who I am?" she asked. The Rabbit looked up at her, and it seemed to him that he had seen her face before, but he couldn't think of where.

"I am the nursery magic Fairy," she said. "I take care of all the playthings that children have loved. When the children don't need them anymore, I turn them into Real."

"Wasn't I Real before?" asked the little Rabbit.

"You were Real to the Boy," the Fairy said, "because he loved you. Now you shall be Real to everyone."

Then the Fairy took the Rabbit up in her arms and flew away with him into the woods.

The woods were beautiful, and the ferns shone like frosted silver. In the clearing the wild rabbits danced, but when they saw the Fairy, they all stopped dancing and stood around in a ring to stare at her.

"I've brought you a new playmate," the Fairy told them. "You must be very kind to him, for he is going to live with you forever and ever!" Then she kissed the little Rabbit again and said, "Run and play, little Rabbit!"

The little Rabbit sat quite still for a moment. He did not know that when the Fairy had kissed him, she had changed him altogether. He might have sat there for a long time, if just then something hadn't tickled his nose, and he lifted his leg to scratch it.

And he found that he actually had hind legs!
Instead of velveteen, he had brown fur, soft and shiny,
and his ears twitched by themselves.

He gave one leap, and the joy of using those hind
legs was so great, he went springing about—jumping
sideways and whirling around as the others did. He
grew so excited that when he did stop to look for the
Fairy, she had gone.

He was a Real Rabbit at last!

Autumn passed, and Winter, and in the Spring, the Boy went out to play in the wood. While he was playing, two rabbits crept out and peeped at him. One of them had strange markings under his fur, as though long ago he had been stuffed.

The Boy thought to himself, "Why, he looks just like my old Bunny that was lost!"

But he never knew that it really was his own Bunny, who had come back to look at the child who had first helped him to be Real.